W9-AYM-543

GAME DAY
BASEBALL
AN INTERACTIVE SPORTS STORY

BY ERIC BRAUN
ILLUSTRATED BY FRAN BUENO

CAPSTONE PRESS
a capstone imprint

You Choose Books are published by Capstone Press, an imprint of Capstone.
1710 Roe Crest Drive
North Mankato, Minnesota 56003
www.capstonepub.com

Library of Congress Cataloging-in-Publication Data
Names: Braun, Eric, 1971- author. | Bueno, Fran, illustrator.
Title: Game day baseball : an interactive sports story / by Eric Braun ;
[illustrated by Fran Bueno].
Description: North Mankato, Minnesota : Capstone Press, [2021] | Series:
You choose: Game day sports | Audience: Ages 8-11. | Audience: Grades
4-6. | Summary: It is the championship baseball game and the reader's
choices can mean the difference between a triumphant victory and a
heartbreaking loss.
Identifiers: LCCN 2020039524 (print) | LCCN 2020039525 (ebook) | ISBN
9781496696014 (hardcover) | ISBN 9781496697103 (paperback) | ISBN
9781977154255 (ebook pdf)
Subjects: LCSH: Plot-your-own stories. | CYAC: Baseball--Fiction. |
Plot-your-own stories.
Classification: LCC PZ7.1.B751542 Gam 2021 (print) | LCC PZ7.1.B751542
(ebook) | DDC [Fic]--dc23
LC record available at https://lccn.loc.gov/2020039524
LC ebook record available at https://lccn.loc.gov/2020039525

Editorial Credits
Editor: Angie Kaelberer; Designer: Kayla Rossow; Media Researcher: Eric Gohl;
Premedia Specialist: Katy LaVigne

TABLE OF CONTENTS

ABOUT YOUR GAME

YOU are a baseball player with a history of practicing hard, playing hard, and making smart choices. You're known for your keen instincts and coming up big in tough situations. Your teammates look up to you, and your coach relies on you. But there's just one thing on your mind—can you lead your team to the tournament championship?

Chapter One sets the scene. Then you choose which path to read. Follow the directions at the bottom of the page as you read the stories. The decisions you make will change your outcome. After you finish one path, go back and read the others for new perspectives and more adventures.

CHAPTER 1

A COMEBACK SEASON

This baseball season has been a wild ride. Your team, the Rockets, started off slow. One of your best hitters missed the first couple of weeks with a sprained ankle and came back rusty. Everyone played as hard as ever, but the hits weren't dropping in and the pitching was cold. You went 4–6 through the first 10 games, and then you lost a heartbreaker to your biggest rival, the Railroaders, in extra innings. You were in fourth place and in danger of missing the Tri-City Tournament, the biggest event of the season.

Many of your teammates were feeling down after that Railroaders game. Even Coach Kowalski said, "Maybe this isn't our year."

Turn the page.

Coach calls you "the Bus" because you have a motormouth—and because sometimes you carry the whole team. You knew you had to say something to encourage your team members to keep trying.

"Come on, guys!" you pleaded. "Don't give up now. We're about to get hot—I can feel it!" Some of the guys nodded. But you could tell they weren't so sure.

Attitudes began to change when you won your next game. The game after that was an extra innings nail-biter, but this time your team came out on top. You followed that with another win. In fact, the Rockets reeled off five victories in a row and took 12 of the last 16 games.

The Tri-City Tournament is right around the corner, and you've made it in. After digging out of that early-season hole, the team believes anything is possible. But one thing is for sure—the Rockets can't afford another slump. That means you'll have to step up your game even more.

It's time to play ball!

To be a slick-fielding shortstop, using your highlight-reel defense to impact the game, turn to page 11.

To be a crafty pitcher, enduring high-stress pressure on the mound, turn to page 45.

To be a wise-but-tough catcher, managing the pitching game and hitting for power, turn to page 73.

CHAPTER 2

FLASHING THE LEATHER

Power hitters get the glory. Pitchers get the spotlight. But no team can be great without great defense. And no defensive position is more important than shortstop. That's where hard grounders come the hardest. That's where tough hops are the toughest. Where smoking line drives are the hottest.

That's where you play. Shortstop for the Rockets—it's where hits go to die, and everyone knows it.

The Rockets draw a tough matchup from a neighboring city in the first round. The Cyclones are known as big hitters. But the Rockets win a tight one, 3–2. In the second round, you blow out the Sun Dogs 8–1.

Turn the page.

Round three is against the Aggies, who score early and are nursing a 2–1 lead in the top of the seventh. With a runner on first and one out, the runner takes off. The pitch is a high fastball that the batter whiffs for strike three. Your catcher, Billy, pops to his feet and fires a perfect throw to you, covering second base. You pluck it just above the bag and slap the tag down—he's out! The play ends the inning, and the Rockets get ready to bat.

Everyone's feeling great. That is, everyone but you. The base runner at second came in hard and gashed your wrist with his spikes. You held on to the ball to get the out, but your wrist is bleeding badly. It's also throbbing with pain. You wrap it in a towel. The Rockets string together four hits and win the game on Billy's two-run double. Thankfully, you don't have to bat.

The win means you're going to the championship game. You celebrate with your teammates, but secretly you're worried. Your wrist is already swollen and stiff. It hurts to move it. You have just two days to heal. Should you tell Coach Kowalski? You don't want to sit out the big game.

To hide the injury, turn to page 14.
To tell Coach Kowalski, turn to page 16.

You keep the injury to yourself. No need to let anyone worry about it.

During the two days before the big game, you rest your wrist. No practicing. No exercise. You don't even play video games.

On game day, the wrist still aches, but it's a lot better. Your biggest worry is batting—will you be able to swing with authority?

It's a beautiful, hot summer day. The bleachers are full of family members, friends, and even a few kids from the neighborhood. Excitement is in the air.

Your opponent in this game is your old rival, the Railroaders. They blasted their way through the first three games of the tournament, scoring a total of 25 runs and allowing only six. They look loose and confident. They're not afraid of you, that's for sure.

They go three up, three down in the top of the first, and you don't have to make any plays. You feel a little relief. Then your team comes up to bat. You bat leadoff and slap an inside pitch down the left-field line for a double. The wrist hurts more, but the crowd's cheering helps you ignore the pain.

Unfortunately, the next three batters strike out, and you're stranded. You come up to bat again in the third inning with Billy on third and two outs. Coach gives you the sign to swing away, but your wrist is killing you. You are not sure if you can put a good swing on the ball. You do think you can lay down a good bunt against this pitcher.

To swing away as instructed, turn to page 18.
To bunt, turn to page 20.

You wait until the dugout has mostly cleared out, and you help Coach Kowalski bag up the bats and helmets. Before you can open your mouth, Coach glances over and notices your wrist. "Hey," he says, "what's with the towel?"

"I got spiked on that play at the bag," you say. "It really hurts."

You unwrap the towel and show him the gash—dried blood caked all over, two deep lines of shredded skin, and a big, swollen bruise. He asks you if it hurts, and you shake your head. It does hurt, but you don't want to admit it.

He gives you instructions to ice the wrist four times a day. He also says to take ibuprofen consistently to reduce the swelling and not to move it. "Rest and ice," he says. "Rest and ice."

You do as you're told. When game day rolls around, you feel a lot better. Not 100 percent, but pretty close. Your opponent in the championship game is the Railroaders, the team that beat you earlier in the season, and you can't wait.

Early in the game, with a runner on first and one out, you get a chance to test your wrist. A hot grounder is hit toward the hole. You dive, spear it on a short hop, and leap to your feet.

Your second baseman, Junior, covers the bag and awaits your throw. A double play would end the inning, but the runner heading toward second is almost there. You're not sure you can get him.

To take the sure out at first, turn to page 22.
To go for the double play, turn to page 25.

If Coach says swing away, then you have to swing away. That's your job. The next pitch is a fastball right down the middle. It's the kind of meatball you'd usually clobber. But because of the sore wrist, you're too slow. You pop it up in foul territory. The first baseman gets under it and makes the catch.

You're out.

In the top half of the fourth inning, the Railroaders' shortstop skims a grounder to your backhand side. You get there in time, but when you squeeze the ball, it pops out. Your wrist buzzes with pain.

Thankfully, the Railroaders don't score. When you get back to the dugout, Coach Kowalski calls you over to talk. "What's going on? You don't look right."

Maybe it's time to confess.

To tell Coach Kowalski about your bad wrist, turn to page 28.

To keep it secret, turn to page 30.

You know you can't get around on the fastball, not with this bad wrist. You might get in trouble for ignoring the sign, but if the bunt is a good one, Coach will forgive you.

The pitcher winds up. You pivot, lower the bat into the zone, and watch the ball all the way in.

Plink!

The ball kisses off the sweet part of the bat and rolls softly down the third-base line. It's a beauty! You drop the bat and run as hard as you can toward first. Out of the corner of your eye, you see the pitcher racing toward the ball. Ahead of you, the first baseman stretches to receive the throw. You make one last long stride toward the bag just as the first baseman makes the catch.

"He's out!"

In the dugout, the coach yells at you in front of everyone. "What was that? You got the swing away sign! We had two outs!"

"Sorry, Coach," you say. "I screwed up. I won't do it again." As you run onto the field, you just hope you'll get a chance to make up for it.

Your chance comes in the bottom of the seventh inning. The game is tied 1–1 when you come up to bat with one out. A kid they call Big Cheese is pitching. His cheese—his fastball—is the best in the league. Big Cheese keeps busting you inside with fastballs, and he's got you down 1 and 2.

You know the next pitch will be another fastball inside. You're not sure you can get to it with the bad wrist. But you might be able to get on base if you lean in just a bit and let it hit you.

To try to get hit by the pitch, turn to page 32.
To swing at it, turn to page 34.

It's better to get at least one out than risk not getting any. So you fire to first base. Easy out.

"Come on!" Junior says to you. "We had this guy." He slaps his glove against his thigh. The runner on second stands up and dusts off his pants.

"Just playing it safe," you tell Junior. Ever since you hurt your wrist, you've been playing cautiously. It's not your style.

The runner on second steals third and scores on a sacrifice fly. It's 0–1, Railroaders.

Back in the dugout, you try to fire up your teammates. "Let's get some hits!" But after two innings, it's still 0–1.

After three innings, it's still 0–1. The scoreless innings pile up. With each one that goes by, you worry a bit more.

It's still 0–1 in the bottom of the seventh—your last chance to score. Things look good when Billy leads off with a single. But Junior grounds into a double play. Two outs. Your pitcher, Max Carey, hits a line drive into center and stands on first base when you come up to bat. It's your big chance.

Adrenaline courses through you. You forget all about your bad wrist. Max takes a big lead off first. The pitcher winds up.

The pitch is over the plate.

You put a big swing on it.

Crack!

It feels good off the bat. The ball flies into deep right field. The right fielder runs back toward the fence. Max races around second, heading for third.

Turn the page.

The right fielder puts his glove up and catches it. You're out.

Game over.

The Rockets fall to the Railroaders by the score of 0–1. And that one run was made by the player you didn't double up in the first inning. You will be thinking about that all winter long.

THE END

To follow another path, turn to page 9.
To learn more about baseball, turn to page 103.

You grab the ball from your glove and quickly flip it to Junior, who steps across the bag and throws hard to first. The throw nips the batter by half a step—double play!

You and Junior exchange a high five as you jog off the field. Your experience and daring paid off.

It's a good thing, too, because nobody scores for almost the entire game. It's still 0–0 when the Rockets get their ups in the bottom of the seventh. Score here, and you win.

The Railroaders bring on a pitcher with a tough curveball. He gets the first two batters to strike out, but you crack a triple to left field.

Turn the page.

After hitting the triple, you stand on third base with the hot sun beating down as your first baseman, Bub, comes up to bat. Bub is an all-or-nothing hitter. He might hit it a mile, sending you to home easily. Or he might strike out and send the game to extra innings. On the first pitch, he swings wildly at a curveball in the dirt.

The pitcher isn't watching you closely, and you take a big lead, thinking that you might be able to make a steal. The count is 2–2, and you think he'll throw another curveball here. That's a slow pitch, and it will probably land in the dirt—hard for the catcher to handle.

To try to steal home and win the game, turn to page 36.
To let Bub try to hit you in, turn to page 38.

"I have to tell you something," you say. "My wrist is hurt—bad."

"When did this happen?" Coach asks.

"Last game," you say.

"And you're just telling me now?" Coach shakes his head. He takes you out of the game and puts José at shortstop. In his first inning in the field, José makes an error, and you feel even worse. The Railroaders get two runs, and your team is down 0–2 going into the seventh inning. But Billy knocks in one with a single, and the next hitter, Bub, walks. With two outs and two runners on base, José comes up to bat. The Rockets are down by just one run.

You hold your breath. There's a reason José is a backup—he's not as good as you. You're sure the Rockets are going to lose now, and it will be your fault.

Instead, José turns on a slider and hits into the left-center gap. Billy scores. Bub scores. Rockets win!

Your teammates run out onto the field. José is beaming with pride. You're happy for him and happy for the team. But part of you is jealous. You wish you'd been a part of it.

While the team is still celebrating, Coach comes up to you. "Take care of that wrist, OK?" he says. "We'll need you for fall ball. It's only a couple of weeks away."

"OK," you say. You almost forgot about fall ball. You can hardly wait.

THE END
To follow another path, turn to page 9.
To learn more about baseball, turn to page 103.

"I'm fine," you say. "Don't worry, Coach. We're gonna win this."

Two innings later, it's still tied 0–0 when a Railroaders batter gets a walk. During the next at bat, the runner at first takes off. Your catcher, Billy, makes a good throw to you. You snag it and lay the tag on the runner's ankle as he slides in.

The tag is in time, but the ball slips out of your glove when you make the tag. Safe.

You pick up the ball and walk it to the mound. "You all right?" Max asks you. You're famous for your good hands.

The runner scores on the next batter's double, putting the Railroaders up 0–1. Back in the dugout, Coach confronts you again. This time he sees your gashed and swollen wrist. He's furious that you weren't honest with him. "Selfish," he says, almost spitting the word.

José replaces you at shortstop and does OK, but a grounder gets past him that you are sure you would have had. All you can do is watch as the Railroaders tack on another run. The innings tick by, and their two-run lead holds up. They win the game.

At least you can play video games now. But that really doesn't make you feel any better about letting your team down. You won't make the same mistake next season.

THE END

To follow another path, turn to page 9.
To learn more about baseball, turn to page 103.

You're not sure if the sore wrist is the reason you're late on the fastball or if it's just worrying about the wrist that's making you hesitate. Or maybe Big Cheese is just too good. Whatever the case, your confidence isn't there.

So you make up your mind to take one for the team. As Big Cheese fires another smoking fastball inside, you lean in just a tiny bit. But the pitch was more inside than you thought. Instead of getting nicked, you get hit hard.

On the wrist.

Your bad wrist.

You drop the bat as pain shoots up your arm. You squeeze your eyes shut. Your knees go weak, but you start jogging toward first base.

When you get there, the base coach gives you a funny look. "You OK?" he asks you. "You're crying."

You realize he's right. Coach Kowalski comes out, takes one look at your face, and says, "You need to get that checked out."

Your mom takes you to the emergency room while the game continues without you. You don't know if the Rockets will win or lose, but you do know one thing. You're going to be more honest in the future.

THE END

To follow another path, turn to page 9.
To learn more about baseball, turn to page 103.

Let yourself get hit by a pitch? No way. You're going to take your cuts.

Big Cheese goes into his windup. You take a deep breath as you load up for a swing. The pitch comes whistling in and you slash at it. Contact!

A grounder skips just inside of first base and rolls toward the right fielder. Your wrist is throbbing with pain, but you ignore it. It's rally time, and you're safe at first base.

The next batter is Bennie, your team's best contact hitter. On a 1–1 count, Coach gives you the steal sign. You add an extra step to your lead. Big Cheese goes into his motion. You take off.

You safely slide into second. Bennie drives the next pitch over the infield into center. You dig hard for third. Coach wheels his arm to signal you to keep running. The catcher steps in front of the plate to receive the throw, but you slide in behind him. Safe!

Rockets win!

As your teammates rush out to celebrate with you, you forget all about your injured wrist. In fact, you never felt so good.

THE END

To follow another path, turn to page 9.
To learn more about baseball, turn to page 103.

You saw the way Bub flailed at the curveball. He's a big-time hitter, but you just don't think he's got this pitcher's number. It's time to take matters into your own hands.

The pitcher stands tall, both feet on the rubber, staring in at the catcher. You set your sights on his feet. As soon as that left foot lifts, you take off.

"He's going!" someone screams.

Dirt flies up behind your cleats with each step. The pitcher steps off the rubber and throws to the catcher. Bub steps out of the box, making room. You dive headfirst. Then you run your fingers across the plate just under the catcher's tag.

Safe!

You score the only run in a 1–0 pitchers' duel, carrying the Rockets to victory. In the end, your wrist didn't make much difference. It was your ice-cold confidence that locked up the win.

THE END

To follow another path, turn to page 9.
To learn more about baseball, turn to page 103.

You decide to play it safe and let Bub hit. Just as you predicted, the pitcher tosses another curveball. Unfortunately, Bub swings over it. Strike three.

The game goes to extra innings, and you sense your teammates are getting tense. Any mistake could cost you the game.

"Stay loose, boys!" yells Coach Kowalski, as if he read your mind.

Nobody scores in the eighth inning. The Railroaders seem as tense as the Rockets do. In the top of the tenth, you're playing in the field when the batter bloops a fly ball behind you. You run back, keeping your eye on the ball. You sense that your left fielder, Paco, is running in hard. But the crowd is yelling, Coach is yelling . . . it's hard to hear. Did Paco say "I got it?" You can't be sure.

To hold up and let Paco catch the fly, turn to page 40.
To handle it yourself, turn to page 42.

You don't want to have a collision, so you pull up.

The ball drops in for a hit, and the batter makes it to second base on the little bloop. "Where were you?" you yell at Paco as you pick up the ball.

"That was yours!" he yells back.

Two batters later, a ground ball scoots just under your glove near second base. The runner on second takes off—he rounds third base and scores. The next batter hits a triple, bringing the runner on first home. The next batter walks, and the batter after that hits another double, scoring two more.

By the time the Rockets come up to bat in the bottom of the tenth inning, you're down 0–5. Everyone is down in the dumps. You go three up, three down.

After the game, Paco gives you a sad fist bump. "My bad, man," he says.

"No," you say. "It was on me. I'm sorry."

THE END

To follow another path, turn to page 9.
To learn more about baseball, turn to page 103.

You keep running back, keep your eye on the ball, and reel in the fly. Paco jogs up and pats you on the back as you head for the dugout.

"Nice play!"

When you get to the dugout, the tone has changed. Instead of feeling tense, your teammates are excited. "Great catch!" someone says. "Now let's get some hits!"

The first batter is Paco, and he hits a single. The next batter grounds out, advancing Paco to second. Next up, Billy singles to right, but Paco has to stop at third because of a good throw from the right fielder.

It's first and third with two outs when you come up to bat. Feeling confident and pumped up, you swing at the first pitch you see. You rip it back up the middle, past the pitcher's outstretched glove, over second base, and into the outfield.

Paco scores the winning run!

THE END
To follow another path, turn to page 9.
To learn more about baseball, turn to page 103.

CHAPTER 3

THE ACE AND THE DEUCE

You're the ace. The number-one pitcher on your team. The guy who everyone wants on the mound when you just *have to* win.

So Coach Kowalski gives you the ball to start the team's first game of the tournament. It's single elimination, which means if you lose, you are out. No pressure.

The afternoon is hot with no wind and no clouds. Earlier in the day, the Railroaders defeated the Bears. Some of the Railroaders' players are in the stands to watch your game. You have a feeling that if you make it to the final game, it's going to be against them. They're the team to beat.

Turn the page.

After giving up a run in the first inning, you settle down, and the Rockets win 3–1. Two days later, your fellow pitcher Max Carey pitches game two, which the Rockets also win. The team's third pitcher, Bennie, starts the third game. This one is all offense, as neither pitcher does especially well. But in the end, the Rockets outslug the Cyclones for the win.

You've made it to the final game. The championship. And your guess was right. Your opponent is the Railroaders. Coach tabs you to start. You've faced this team before. They are a very good hitting team. They're dangerous.

Your job is to shut them down. You'll do it with your hard fastball and a cutter that darts toward the right batter's box. You also have a curveball that you can throw for strikes—a nasty weapon.

Unlike the last time you pitched, the weather feels like fall. It's cool. It's also a night game, adding extra chill to the air. Your hands are cold, and you can't get a good grip on the curveball. You're not getting strikes. You sandwich two walks around a strikeout. With runners on first and second, their cleanup hitter knocks a booming double. Both runners score.

Turn the page.

After the inning, your catcher, Billy, sits next to you on the bench. "What's up with the deuce?" That's what he calls the curveball—the sign for a curve is two fingers.

"Cold hands," you say.

"Shoot," Billy says. "Think we should scrap it?"

Without the curveball, you only have two pitches. It would be enough to beat many teams. But maybe not this one.

To scrap the curveball, go to page 49.
To keep trying it, turn to page 52.

The score is 0–2 as you take the mound in the top of the second. Relying only on your fastball and cutter, you get two strikeouts and a weak pop-up.

"You make it look easy," Billy says back in the dugout. You just smile—yeah, easy.

You pitch a scoreless third inning too. But the fourth opens with two straight hits. You get the next batter to chase the high cheese for strike three, the first out of the inning. But the batters are starting to catch up to your fastball. Not having to worry about the curve makes it easier for them.

Turn the page.

Next up is a big lefty named Sid. This guy has feasted on your cutter. So you don't give him any of those. Using all fastballs, you get to a full count, 3–2. He's sitting on that fastball now. He knows that's all you've got. If you throw another one, he'll be ready.

On the other hand, you've warmed up nicely now. Your grip feels strong. You think you might be able to throw that curveball now.

To try to get a fastball past him, turn to page 54.
To surprise him with the curveball, turn to page 56.

In the second inning, things start off badly again. You walk the first batter, with ball four coming on a curveball that drops in the dirt in front of the plate. You get a quick out on a fly to right field. Then the next batter singles. With runners at the corners, you strike out the Railroaders' pitcher with a cutter.

The next batter hits a dribbler off your curve. You hustle to make the play, but your throw to first is a hair late. He's safe, and the runner on third scores. That makes it 0–3.

Billy visits you on the mound. This game is about to get out of control. You think Billy is going to tell you no more curveballs. Instead, he says, "He barely made contact on that. It was a good pitch."

"Yeah," you agree.

"But the next batter is Jonathan." A tall, skinny player with freckles and long red hair is coming to bat. You've faced him many times. And for some reason, you can never strike him out.

"We can walk him," Billy says. "We have an open base. Put him on and face the next guy."

The next guy is their shortstop, a good fielder but not much of a hitter. Definitely an easier out.

To intentionally walk Jonathan, turn to page 58.
To pitch to him, turn to page 60.

This is no time to experiment with a curveball you *think* you can throw well. Sid wiggles his bat in anticipation. You reach back and throw your hardest fastball.

Sid unleashes a mighty swing and swats the ball deep into right-center field. It clangs off the fence as both the base runners score. Your heart sinks. It's 0–4. Runner on second, one out.

As you get ready to face the next batter, Sid starts dancing off second base. You look back. He's smiling at you. Daring you to throw him out. Your second baseman, Junior, shades a bit closer to the bag. He's ready for the throw.

You whip around and try to pick off the runner. But your throw is low and skips past Junior into center field. Sid advances easily to third base.

There's still only one out. You look over, and Sid is really smiling now. The next batter grounds out to first, but Sid scores on the play. It's now 0–5.

The Rockets get two runs back in the bottom of the fourth, and two more in the fifth. In the seventh inning, the Rockets are still down by one run when Sid steps up to bat again. He's wearing that big smile as if he just *knows* he's going to get a hit.

You could wipe that smile off his face. All you have to do is hit him with a fastball. He would get to take first base. But there are two outs and nobody else on base. You can get the next guy out.

To hit him, turn to page 63.

To pitch to him normally, turn to page 65.

Your curveball comes in spinning like a top and drops like a bowling ball. Sid, who was definitely expecting the fastball, swings right over it. The umpire calls it out: "Steee-rike three!"

Later, the Rockets grab a couple of runs, and going into the sixth inning, the game is tied at two. Your arm is getting tired, and you give up a hit but get two outs. That's when Sid comes up to bat again.

On a 3–0 count, Sid gets ahold of a fastball. The sound of the ball off his bat is like two bricks clapping together—*smack!*

You turn and watch it fly toward the fence. It's deep. Your right fielder, Jack, is racing back. Your heart feels like concrete in your chest. But Jack makes the catch on the run, right in front of the fence.

Nothing but a long, scary out.

Back in the dugout, some of the guys are putting on batting helmets and batting gloves when Coach Kowalski puts his hand on your shoulder. "How do you feel?" he asks.

You're tired, but you don't want to come out of the game. You want to be a part of this.

To tell him you're fine, turn to page 66.
To let him know you're tired, turn to page 68.

Walking Jonathan will be humiliating—everyone will think you're afraid of him. But it's the smart thing to do.

You walk him intentionally. As Jonathan takes his base, he looks at you. "Chicken, huh?"

Your face burns with embarrassment, but you funnel your anger into striking out the next batter on three straight pitches. Jonathan is left standing on first. The walk paid off.

After that, the Rockets start to hit. It's about time! You get two runs in the third and two in the sixth. Better yet, you have kept the Railroaders off the board since the second inning. Your curveball started biting, and they haven't been able to touch it. The seventh inning rolls around with the Rockets up 4–3. All you have to do is get three outs, and you win.

But the autumn wind has picked up, and it's getting hard to keep your hand warm. You get a strikeout but give up a hit and two walks. It's bases loaded with one out.

And who's coming up to bat? It's Jonathan, of course. And this time, you can't walk him. That would tie the game.

You have an excellent infield. If Jonathan hits a grounder, they may be able to turn a double play. That would end the game—and win it.

You could try to strike him out. If you can do that, you'd still need one more out. But the light-hitting shortstop is next.

To try for the double play, turn to page 69.
To go for the strikeout, turn to page 71.

You're not backing down from a challenge. "Let's get him," you say.

Billy nods. "Let's do it."

It starts off well. You get Jonathan to swing and miss on a curve, then you get a called strike on a chest-high fastball. Billy calls for a fastball next. You rock and fire. And Jonathan smacks it. Hard.

The runner on second scores easily, making it 0–4 Railroaders. You strike out the shortstop after that, and the Rockets score a run in their half of the inning. You go back out to pitch the third inning, and Billy was right about your curveball. It's back. You breeze through the third, fourth, and fifth innings.

The Rockets score two more, and you're losing 3–4 in the bottom of the seventh inning. Your last chance.

You come up with a runner on second base and lace a slider into the gap in right field. An easy double. The runner ahead of you scores. Tie game. Then, as you're approaching second, the center fielder bobbles the ball. You don't hesitate. You round second and dig for third. The center fielder makes a good throw, but you slide in under the tag.

Turn the page.

The next two batters strike out, but Billy comes up and singles up the middle. You trot home easily. Your aggressive playing led to you scoring the winning run. You can't wait to celebrate with your teammates.

THE END

To follow another path, turn to page 9.
To learn more about baseball, turn to page 103.

Sid really makes you mad. Always grinning when he beats you. It's time to send a message. So you wind up and throw your hardest fastball. It hits him in the ribs, and he collapses to the ground, the wind knocked out of him. His coach comes out to check on him. As you stand there watching, all your anger turns to guilt. What were you thinking? Hitting a batter? That's not who you are.

Sid finally gets up and jogs to first base. For once, he doesn't look at you.

Your focus has been rattled. You give up a walk and a hit, and Sid scores. Ugh. Now you're down by two runs. Coach Kowalski calls you into the dugout. He says, "Did you hit him on purpose?" When you don't answer, he shakes his head. He looks so disappointed.

Turn the page.

Coach brings in Bennie to pitch. He does OK, but the Rockets score only one in the bottom of the seventh. Your team loses by one.

After the game, when you line up to shake hands, every single Railroaders player pulls his hand back when you come by. They won't shake hands with you.

THE END

To follow another path, turn to page 9.
To learn more about baseball, turn to page 103.

Sure, Sid is frustrating. He's not a good sport. But if you hit him with a pitch, you could hurt him. That's not the kind of person you want to be.

So you toss a curveball for a called strike. He lets a low fastball go by for ball one. Then you burn him with another fastball. With the count at 1–2, you go back to the curveball. It comes in looking juicy, like it's right down the middle, but as he swings, it darts down and away. He misses. Strike three.

The Rockets tie the game 5–5 in the bottom of the seventh, and it goes to extra innings. Bennie pitches a perfect eighth inning for your team, and in the bottom half, the Railroaders bring a reliever of their own. It's Sid! The Rockets rally a run off him, and you get the winning hit. Now *that* feels good.

THE END
To follow another path, turn to page 9.
To learn more about baseball, turn to page 103.

"I feel great," you say. You must sound convincing, because he sends you out to pitch the seventh.

The first batter gets a hit on a fastball. You walk the next batter. You get a groundout, and the runners move up to second and third. Your arm feels like rubber. You walk the next batter.

Billy comes out to the mound. "I'm out of gas," you tell him. Coach brings in Bennie to relieve you, and you feel bad about the situation you've left him with—bases loaded, one out.

Bennie strikes out their center fielder, a good hitter. You relax a bit. But the next batter bloops a lucky single, and two runs score. The Rockets are down by two runs going into the bottom of the last inning. And they don't score any.

Your arm is going to be very sore tomorrow. It will be a painful reminder of how you cost your team two runs because you were too selfish to come out of the game.

THE END

To follow another path, turn to page 9.
To learn more about baseball, turn to page 103.

"I'm running out of steam," you admit.

Coach pats you on the back. "You pitched a great game."

The Rockets can't score in the bottom of the sixth, and Bennie goes out to pitch the top of the seventh. He's throwing so hard, you can hear Billy's catcher's mitt popping. The Railroaders can't touch him. You made the right choice.

The game stays tied until Jack smacks a home run in the bottom of the eighth. You and your teammates meet him as he crosses home plate and you celebrate your first championship!

THE END

To follow another path, turn to page 9.
To learn more about baseball, turn to page 103.

You decide to trust your teammates. Get the ground ball and let them twist the double play.

Jonathan digs in with his back foot. He looks out at you, waiting. You throw a fastball, low and inside. He lets it go. Your next fastball is just a touch higher, and he swings. Just like you planned, it's on the ground. It skips like a stone across a smooth lake, and your shortstop picks it. Quick and smooth, he fires hard to second base.

Junior, the second baseman, receives the throw and turns toward first. He rifles the ball across to Bub at first base, who reaches out to make the catch half a step before Jonathan gets to the bag.

"Yeah!" you yell. Double play. Game over.

Turn the page.

You line up and meet the Railroader players near home plate to shake. Jonathan grabs your hand and shakes it. "Good game," he says.

"You too," you reply.

"But you know what?" he adds. "I'll get you next time."

THE END

To follow another path, turn to page 9.
To learn more about baseball, turn to page 103.

Even if you get the ground ball, the double play isn't guaranteed. There's too much that can go wrong. Better to take care of this yourself. You're going for the strikeout.

You get ahead of the batter 1–2, and Billy calls for a curveball. You throw it, and Jonathan barely gets ahold of it. It flares toward deep short and deflects off the shortstop's glove. The runner on third scores, and the Railroaders tie it up.

You get out of the inning, but the Rockets don't score in the bottom of the seventh. The Railroaders end up winning in extra innings. You feel bad about the loss. But you went after Jonathan the right way. Sometimes people get lucky. You figure you can live with that.

THE END

To follow another path, turn to page 9.
To learn more about baseball, turn to page 103.

CHAPTER 4

THE VIEW FROM BEHIND THE PLATE

Catcher—that's the most important position in the game. At least that's your opinion.

It's the most fun too. Other fielders might get to handle the ball a few times per game, but you touch the ball on almost every pitch. You give the signs that tell the pitcher what to throw. You study batters for their weaknesses. You squat behind the plate and see the whole field. It's like you're a king looking over his kingdom.

The pitchers on the Rockets love pitching to you because you call a good game. You block all those pitches in the dirt. You don't just help them look good—you help them *be* good. Sometimes great.

Turn the page.

Of course, defense is only one half of the game. You also love the other half—hitting. You're not the best hitter on the team, but you have power.

Your team starts the Tri-City Tournament with some serious momentum. You roll through the first three rounds and make it to the final game. The championship. You'll be facing the Railroaders. They had the best record in the league, and if you asked them, they'd say they are the best team. They expect to win.

Of course, you didn't ask them. The only opinion that matters is yours and that of the other Rockets. Forget the regular season. The Rockets are the best, and you're ready to prove it.

For the big game, Coach Kowalski tabs Joey Basil to pitch—or, as you call him, Bazooka Joe. He has an arm like a cannon.

"Let's blow them away," you tell Joey.

In the first inning, Joey gets three quick outs. In the bottom of the inning, you come up to bat second. There's a runner on first and no outs. You smack a liner into right center and round first. As you look out, you see the right fielder picking up the ball deep in right field. You know he has a good arm, but you think you can stretch this into a double.

To go for second, turn to page 76.
To hold up at first, turn to page 78.

You turn the corner and hoof it for second. The second baseman straddles the bag and catches the throw from right field. You come in sliding, but he gets the tag down in time. You're out.

You jog off the field, where Coach Kowalski snaps at you. "Nobody out. First inning. We don't take silly chances in that situation."

You know he's right. You let your emotions get the best of you. You were too excited. "Sorry, Coach," you say. "I'll make it up."

The next few innings go by in a blur. Both pitchers are throwing well, and there isn't any scoring. You're calling a great game behind the plate, and Bazooka Joe hasn't even allowed a base hit.

You come up in the bottom of the fourth with a runner on third base and a chance to knock in the game's first run. The pitcher is pitching you very carefully. No more fat strikes—everything is off the plate. You work the count to three balls and no strikes.

The next pitch comes in high. You know it's ball four. But you also know that if you can get ahold of it, you'll hit it very far. Is it too high to hit?

To swing away, turn to page 80.
To take the walk, turn to page 82.

You take a wide turn at first but slow up. The throw comes in hard from the right fielder. You made a smart choice staying put—you would have been out.

Batting after you is your big first baseman, Bub. He cracks a hard grounder through the right side. Your teammate is thrown out at home. You advance to third. The next batter strikes out. Up next, Bazooka Joe grounds out. But you score the first run of the game on the play.

The Railroaders tie it at one in the top of the fifth. As your team bats in the bottom of the fifth, you watch the other team's pitcher closely. His name is Chance, and you've faced him before. But you notice something now that you never noticed before. Sometimes when he's standing in the set, about to pitch, he seems to move his hand around inside his glove. It looks as if he's trying to get the right grip before he throws. You watch him several pitches in a row. Each time he does it, he throws a curveball.

You're *almost* sure of it.

Do you tell your teammates? If they can know when the curveball is coming, it would help them a lot. But if you're wrong, it could really mess them up.

To tell someone about the tip, turn to page 85.
To keep it to yourself, turn to page 87.

You can't resist the high fastball. You know you can clobber it. So you swing away. And you make contact.

Unfortunately, you get just under it. A weak pop fly floats over the infield. The second baseman calls for it and catches it. The inning ends without a score.

In the top of the fifth, the Railroaders' speedy center fielder comes up to bat. He works a 3–1 count. He steps out of the box and looks down to his coach in the box by third base. The coach goes through a long set of signs. You've been watching him the entire game, and most of his signs are simple. Could the longer string of signs mean he's putting on some kind of special play?

Then you remember playing the Railroaders a few weeks ago. This center fielder bunted *twice* in that game. He's a good bunter. Is he going to bunt now?

If you call for a high fastball, you might be able to make him bunt it straight up into the air. Then you can catch it for an easy out. But if he doesn't go for it, it will be a walk.

To call for the high fastball, turn to page 90.
To call something else, turn to page 92.

You were taught not to swing at bad pitches. Even though you're hungry to get a hit here, you know your best bet is to take the ball.

The ump tells you to take your base, and you trot down the baseline to first. The next hitter gets a single and the runner on third scores. The Rockets take the lead, 1–0. Your patience paid off.

It's 1–1 when you lead off the bottom of the seventh. Once again, the pitcher is careful not to give you anything good to hit. You get another walk, representing the winning run as you stand on first base. The first-base coach gives you a fist bump. "That a way! Let's win this thing now."

Turn the page.

Sounds good to you. There are two outs, and your first baseman, Bub, digs into the batter's box. On a 2–2 count, he slices a liner into the right-field corner. You get a good jump and are rounding second base in a hurry. You're chugging toward third with a full head of steam. Coach Kowalski is coaching third base. At the last second, he puts up the stop sign. But you're going hard.

To stop at third, turn to page 94.
To ignore Coach's sign and go home, turn to page 96.

Your left fielder is in the hole, and you grab his shoulder. "Paco," you say. "See how he's rooting around in his glove right now?"

"Sure," Paco says.

"He's getting his curveball grip. Watch." Sure enough, the next pitch is a curveball. Bub swings and misses. You and Paco watch a couple more pitches. When Chance throws the fastball, he reaches into his glove and grabs the ball easily. When he throws the curve, he takes an extra couple of seconds to get a good grip.

When Paco goes up to bat, you tell the rest of the guys about the tip. You all watch as Paco lets two curves drop into the dirt for balls. When a fastball comes, he crushes it for a triple.

Turn the page.

The Rockets rally for three runs that inning. The Railroaders bring in a reliever, but by then it's too late. The Rockets hold on for the win.

"Great game," Coach says to you afterward. You got a couple of hits. You called a good game behind the plate. But your biggest contribution might have been just paying attention.

THE END

To follow another path, turn to page 9.
To learn more about baseball, turn to page 103.

You can't be sure, so you decide to keep it to yourself. The Rockets don't end up scoring that inning—and Paco, your left fielder, strikes out on a curveball that you definitely could tell was coming. But it's too late now, because the Railroaders tack on a run in the top of the sixth to take the lead. In the bottom of the inning, they bring in a new pitcher. He doesn't even throw a curveball.

In the top of the seventh, the Railroaders load the bases with two outs. Their biggest slugger, a first baseman named Sid, steps up to bat. If he gets a hit here, at least two runners will score. You are only down by one run now.

Turn the page.

Unfortunately, Bazooka Joe throws two curveballs outside. You put down the sign for a fastball—also called the big cheese—but Joe shakes you off. You do *not* want to go to 3 and 0 on him. So you walk out to talk to Joe.

"I'm not throwing him the cheese," Joe says when you get there. "He got two hits off my fastball today."

To try to convince him to throw the fastball, turn to page 98.

To let him throw curves, turn to page 101.

You're convinced this guy is going to bunt, so you put down a single finger—the sign for a fastball. Then you bounce your glove upward a couple of times to indicate you want it up. You settle your glove nice and high to receive the throw.

Bazooka Joe winds and fires. The batter squares around to bunt, just like you thought he would. The fastball comes in hot and high, just how you wanted it. But it's a little *too* high, and the batter pulls back his bat. Ball four.

He takes his base, and on Joe's very next pitch, he steals second. You try to throw him out, but you're not even close—he's too fast.

Joe strikes out the next batter, and there are two down. Maybe you'll get out of this. But the next batter hits a bloop single just over your shortstop's head. The runner on second motors around third and scores.

Nobody scores the rest of the game. You end up losing the championship 1–0, and you feel responsible. You see Joe walking to the parking lot after the game, and you catch up to him.

"You pitched a gem, Joe," you say. "I'm sorry about that run. It was my fault."

You'll get over it eventually. It just might take until next year's tournament, though.

THE END

To follow another path, turn to page 9.
To learn more about baseball, turn to page 103.

You don't want to risk the walk, so you call for another curveball, and Joe delivers a good one. The batter does square to bunt, but he fouls it into the plate.

On the next pitch, Joe blows him away with a fastball—inning over.

The score remains tied at zero through the seventh inning, and you go to extra innings. In the top of the eighth, the Railroaders score one. You come up to bat in the bottom half of the inning with two outs and a runner on second. Here's your chance to make up for all your mistakes. The out you made at second base. The walk you gave away by popping out on ball four.

Once again you work a 3–0 count, and you lick your lips. He's gotta come after you with a fastball down the middle—he needs a strike.

Here it comes. It's a little high again. You should let it go and take your base. But . . . *nah.*

You rip it deep into left field.

Really deep.

The left fielder is running back. He's at the fence. He's looking up.

He's *still* looking up.

He doesn't even lift his glove. That ball is gone.

Home run.

A *game-winning* home run, to be exact. A championship-winning home run!

THE END
To follow another path, turn to page 9.
To learn more about baseball, turn to page 103.

You stutter-step to a halt just past the bag and dash back to get safe. The throw comes in off-line, and the pitcher has to scramble toward the first-base line to get it.

You would have been safe at home. You're sure of it.

Your second baseman, Junior, grounds out to the pitcher, and the inning is over. You're going to extra innings.

José comes on to relieve Bazooka Joe. He's throwing hard, but he walks two batters. One of them comes around to score.

In the bottom of the eighth, you need a run to tie and two runs to win. The Railroaders bring in a relief pitcher. But unlike José, his control is good. He takes down three hitters in a row— groundout, strikeout, pop out.

You are standing in the on-deck circle with your bat when the game ends. You would have been next up. But you won't get your chance to make a difference. You should have taken the chance last inning, when you had one. Even so, you're proud of your team and how it played.

THE END

To follow another path, turn to page 9.
To learn more about baseball, turn to page 103.

You run through the sign and chug for home. The Railroaders' pitcher screams, "He's going home!" He sounds worried. You smile as you close in.

The pitcher receives the throw on one hop and turns toward home. The catcher moves on top of the plate with his glove out. Out of the corner of your eye, you see fans in the bleachers standing up to get a good view of the play at the plate.

The catcher gets the throw from the pitcher and turns to you. You fling yourself into a feetfirst slide. The catcher's glove comes down, fast and hard.

Your foot scrapes across the plate.

The tag comes down.

The catcher holds up his glove to the umpire to show him he still has the ball. But he was too late. You got in ahead of the tag. The fans in the bleachers are cheering even before the ump makes the call: "SAFE!"

THE END

To follow another path, turn to page 9.
To learn more about baseball, turn to page 103.

"Trust me," you say. "Let's challenge him."

Back behind the plate, you put down the sign for a fastball and set up inside. Sid is ready for it, but he pulls it foul. You call for another one in the same spot. Sid rips this one foul too. You get strike three on a heater high and outside.

Joe pumps his fist—that's a big out!

It seems to change the feeling of the game. Joe leads off for the Rockets in the bottom of the inning and slams a double. Paco bunts him to third.

The Railroaders' coach brings Sid over from first base to pitch. Not only is he a big, hard hitter, but he's also a hard thrower.

Turn the page.

Sid quickly strikes out Junior, and you step to the plate with the game on the line. A hit will win it.

And that's just what happens. You and your teammates hug and cheer as you celebrate the winning run!

THE END

To follow another path, turn to page 9.
To learn more about baseball, turn to page 103.

You don't want to walk in a run. But if your pitcher doesn't feel comfortable with the fastball, you don't want to argue.

You go back behind the plate. Joe throws the curve, and it's ball three. He throws another one for ball four. That walks in a run and increases the Railroaders' lead to two.

The next batter hits a soft grounder to first base, and Bub scoops it up and steps on the bag. You're out of the inning.

The Railroaders bring in a relief pitcher to finish the game. It's Sid. He throws hard and a little wild. With a walk, a stolen base, and a base hit, you manage to get one run back. But that's all you can do, and you end up losing the game by one. That walked-in run was the backbreaker.

THE END
To follow another path, turn to page 9.
To learn more about baseball, turn to page 103.

CHAPTER 5

AMERICA'S NATIONAL PASTIME

Baseball was the first professional sport to become popular in the United States and is nicknamed "America's National Pastime." Two nine-player teams play on a large field marked with four bases arranged in a diamond shape. Teams take turns hitting a pitched ball with a bat at home plate and then running around the bases in order to score a run. Players on the opposing team attempt to get the batters or base runners out, or taken out of play. Each team gets a turn batting during each of the nine innings, and the team with the most runs at the end of the game is the winner.

Baseball likely developed from two British games called rounders and cricket. In both games, players hit a hard ball with a stick or bat. Emigrants from Great Britain brought these and other games to the United States during the 1700s.

The modern game of baseball began in New York City. Members of men's social clubs such as the Gotham Club and the New York Knickerbockers wrote rules for the game. These rules established the diamond-shaped infield and three-strike rule. The first official "baseball" game was played in 1846, when the Knickerbocker Baseball Club played a team of cricket players.

In 1857, the Knickerbockers and 15 other New York clubs created the first organization to govern the sport. The National Association of Base Ball Players (NABBP) also established the first baseball championship. The NABBP created a professional category in 1869. By this time, baseball mostly resembled the game as it's played now.

In 1876, eight professional teams formed the National League. The American League formed in 1901, and Major League Baseball (MLB) was born. Two years later, champion teams from each league met in the first World Series.

In 2020, MLB included 30 teams—15 in each league. Today, thousands of fans attend games in huge stadiums. It's still America's national pastime.

GLOSSARY

bloop (BLOOP)—a softly hit fly ball that drops behind the infield for a hit

bunt (BUHNT)—when the batter gently taps the ball with the bat without swinging

cutter (KUH-tur)—a fastball that breaks toward the pitcher's glove-hand side as it reaches home plate

deuce (DOOSS)—a nickname for a curveball

double play (DUH-buhl PLAY)—when the defense gets two outs on the same play

dribbler (DRIH-blur)—a ball that is hit softly on the ground in the infield

heater (HEE-tur)—a nickname for a fastball

sacrifice fly (SAK-ruh-fisse FLYE)—when a batter hits a fly ball deep enough that a runner can advance a base after the ball is caught; the batter makes an out, "sacrificing" himself in order to help the runner

slider (SLY-duhr)—a fast pitch with a slight curve in the opposite direction of the throwing arm

tip (TIP)—when a pitcher accidentally gives away a clue about the pitch he or she is going to throw

triple (TRIP-uhl)—a hit that allows the batter to reach third base

TEST YOUR BASEBALL KNOWLEDGE

1. What does RBI stand for?

    A. Real Baseball Institute

    B. Runs batted in

    C. Runner bunted in

2. What's the name of the Major League Baseball Championship?

    A. MLB Cup

    B. World Cup

    C. World Series

3. "The Great Bambino" is a nickname for which baseball icon?

    A. Babe Ruth

    B. Joe DiMaggio

    C. Mike Trout

4. What base can you never steal?

    A. first base

    B. third base

    C. home

5. Which of the following is not a nickname for a curveball?

    A. the deuce

    B. Uncle Charlie

    C. the stink

6. How many players take the field on a baseball team?

    A. seven

    B. nine

    C. ten

7. What song do fans sing during the seventh-inning stretch?

    A. "Take Me Out to the Ballgame"

    B. "Closing Time"

    C. "Batter Up"

8. What is it called when two base runners steal a base on the same play?

    A. trick steal

    B. double steal

    C. stealy Dan

9. What do you call someone who can bat left-handed or right-handed?

    A. switch-hitter

    B. flip-hitter

    C. hot stick

10. What does it mean when a batter is "on deck"?

    A. He or she has been hitting really well.

    B. He or she is up to bat.

    C. He or she is next to bat.

DISCUSSION QUESTIONS

>>> What is your favorite sport to play or to watch? Name three things that make it your favorite.

>>> In the book, the narrator has to make decisions about whether or not to stay in the game. What would you have done during these situations? Why?

>>> Many amateur and professional teams have one "star" player. Others have a group of average players who work together really well during the games. Which type of team do you think would be more successful? Why?

AUTHOR BIOGRAPHY

Eric Braun is the author of books on many awesome topics, including dinosaurs, astronauts, true daring escapes, and fractured fairy tales, but baseball is his true love. He never hit for much power, but he knew how to steal a base. Find more of his books at heyericbraun.com.

ILLUSTRATOR BIOGRAPHY

Fran Bueno was born and lives in Santiago de Compostela in Spain. Since he was a little kid, he has loved comic books. He was reading *El Jabato* at age eight, a comic book that his father always bought him, and in that exact moment he decided to become an artist. He studied at art school and will always be grateful to his parents for supporting him. His motivation is to do what he does best and enjoys most. He loves traveling with his wife and kids, being with friends, books, music, movies, and TV shows. Just a regular guy? He would agree.

CHECK OUT ALL 4 BOOKS IN THIS SERIES!

YOU CHOOSE

GAME DAY
BASKETBALL

47 CHOICES
20 ENDINGS

by Brandon Terrell

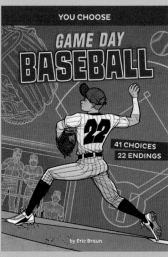

YOU CHOOSE

GAME DAY
BASEBALL

41 CHOICES
22 ENDINGS

by Eric Braun

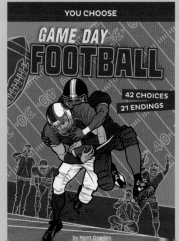

YOU CHOOSE

GAME DAY
FOOTBALL

42 CHOICES
21 ENDINGS

by Matt Doeden

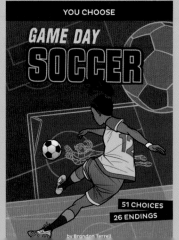

YOU CHOOSE

GAME DAY
SOCCER

51 CHOICES
26 ENDINGS

by Brandon Terrell